Bristl
and the Big Clean

Illustrations by Niall Harding

EGMONT

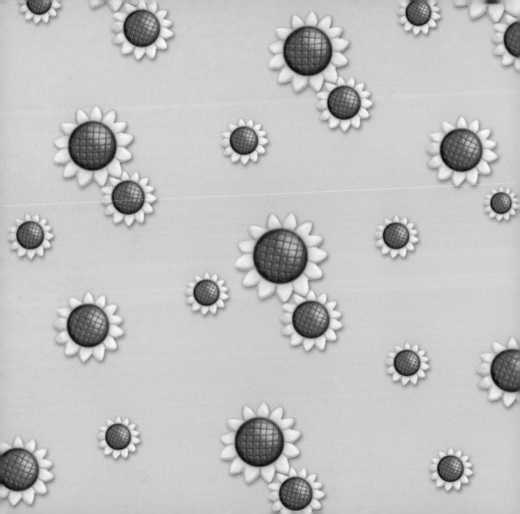

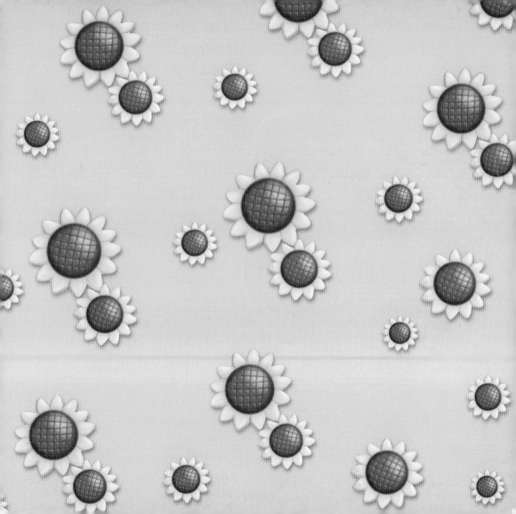

EGMONT

We bring stories to life

First published in Great Britain 2009 by Egmont UK Limited
The Yellow Building, 1 Nicholas Road, London W11 4AN

Endpapers and introductory illustrations by Craig Cameron.

HiT entertainment

ISBN 978 1 4052 4629 3

46329/2

Printed in Italy

FSC
www.fsc.org
MIX
Paper from
responsible sources
FSC® C018306

Bristle, the street sweeper, can't wait to make Bobland Bay spick and span! But is the new member of the team a little too keen to clean?

It was morning. Wendy and Bob were telling the team about a very special job.

"It's the Grand Opening of the Bobland Bay Promenade tonight," said Wendy. "We're going to put up lots of brightly coloured lights and Mayor Bentley will switch them on!"

Suddenly, the team heard a whistle! Along came a little silver and blue machine with red and white brushes and a friendly smile.

"I'm Bristle, the 'Clean as a Whistle' cleaning machine!" said the new arrival cheerfully to the team.

"Your brushes are brilliant!" laughed Dizzy, admiring the fuzzy bristles.

"Thanks," chuckled Bristle. "I've got squirters too – look!" With a whistle, Bristle squirted water at a puddle of mud that Muck had dripped on the ground.

"Ha, ha!" laughed Muck. "I make things all mucky and you get them clean again!"

Bristle looked at Wendy and Bob. "Does this mean I'm part of the team?" he asked.

"Oh, yes!" laughed Wendy. "If there's one thing Bobland Bay needs, it's a machine to keep it clean!"

"You can rely on me!" beamed Bristle proudly. "I'll soon have the place clean as a whistle!"

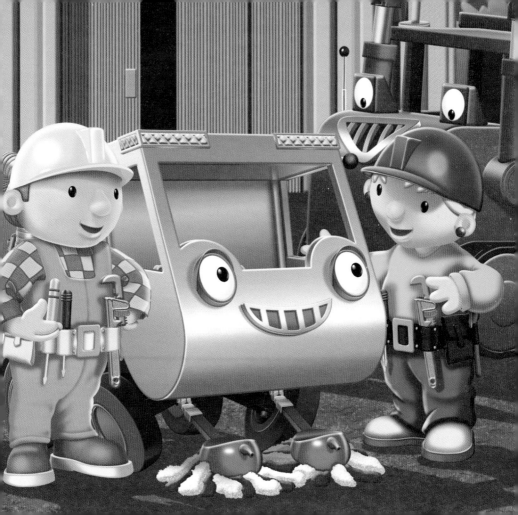

Later, Wendy and the machines were on the promenade. Flex lifted Wendy up so she could paint the lampposts.

Bristle scooted along the promenade, sweeping as he went. "Spick and span! Spick and span!" he sang.

Scoop's job was to scoop up a big pile of sand. He turned away to tip a load into Muck's tipper, but when he turned back, the rest of the sand had gone!

When Wendy had finished painting the lampposts, Flex lowered her to the ground, and she began to paint the railings.

But when she turned round to put more paint on her brush, the paint tin had disappeared! She looked around – but it was nowhere to be seen.

"Oh dear!" gasped Wendy. She pulled out her mobile phone and called Bob to tell him about the missing paint.

Bob soon arrived with more paint for Wendy, and the fairy lights for the promenade. But the moment Bob put the lights down, they disappeared, too!

Suddenly, Bruce the shopkeeper raced over from his shop.

"Nobody move! There's been a robbery!" Bruce cried. He showed Bob the empty space where his display of buckets and spades had been.

"It's a mystery," said Bruce, "that's what it is!"

But Bob had had a brilliant thought. "Everything that disappeared was on the ground! I think I might have solved our little puzzle."

Bruce followed Bob to the edge of the parade of shops. There, they found Bristle fast asleep and snoring loudly!

Bristle woke with a start. "Sorry, Bob! I must have dropped off. I've been rushed off my brushes!" he blustered.

Bob opened Bristle's hatch. Out fell the sand, the lights, Wendy's paint tin and Bruce's buckets and spades!

"Oh, Bristle, you've cleaned up the whole of Bobland Bay!" Bob chuckled.

"I'm sorry," Bristle blushed. "I thought those things needed to be cleaned up!"

"Ha, ha, tidied up and clean as a whistle, eh, Bristle?" laughed Scoop.

"It might be a good idea to ask if things are finished with next time!" laughed Bob. "Come on team, let's get these lights up before the sun goes down. Can we fix it?"

"Yes, we can!" cheered the team.
"Er, yeah, I think so!" added Lofty.

Flex lifted Wendy up to hang the lights and soon, the promenade was ready!

As the sun set, Bob, Wendy and the team gathered on the promenade for the Grand Opening. Mayor Bentley took his place behind the podium, ready to make his speech and switch on the Bobland Bay lights.

But the poor Mayor looked very nervous. He patted his pockets and looked around him. "Oh dear," he mumbled. "I must have dropped my speech!"

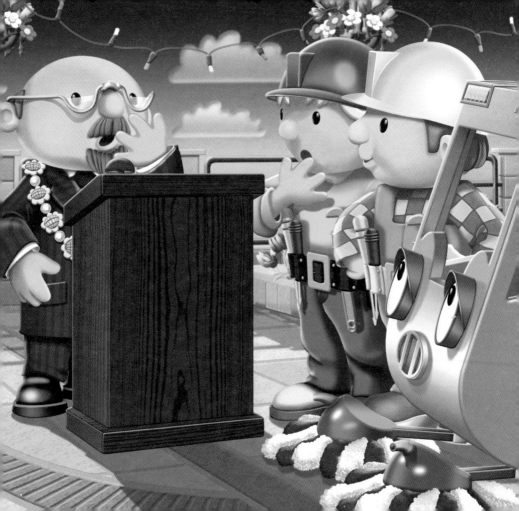

Suddenly, Bristle spotted a piece of paper. He quickly raced after it.

"My speech!" cried Mayor Bentley.

"You can't get away from Bristle!" the little machine whistled, trying to catch the runaway paper. Finally, he managed to sweep it up with his bristly brushes!

"Good work, Bristle!" smiled Bob, as he took the speech out of Bristle's hatch and gave it back to Mayor Bentley.

At last, the Mayor could make his speech. "It gives me great pleasure to declare Bobland Bay Promenade OPEN!"

Mayor Bentley pressed the switch. All along the promenade, the lights glowed brightly. Everyone in Bobland Bay clapped.

"Oh! Wow! They're beautiful!" the machines all cheered …

All except Bristle. "Spick and span!" he whistled, squirting away a spot of mud.

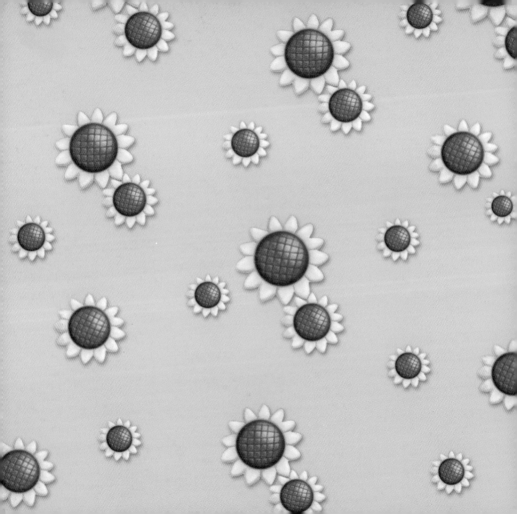

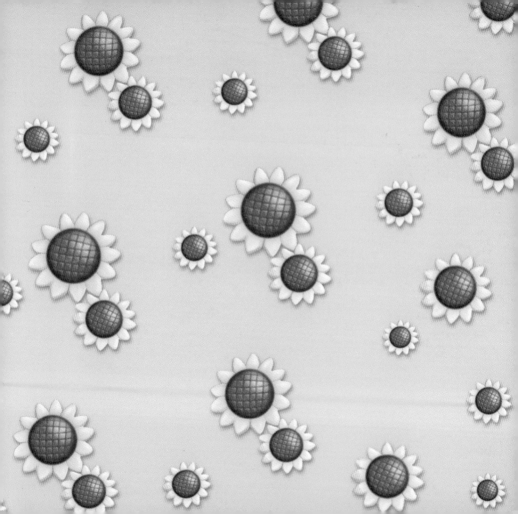